It's Wesley!
The Adirondack Guide

N. Laurie Clark

It's Wesley! The Adirondack Guide

Copyright @ 1998 By N. Laurie Clark, author & illustrator.

Clark Publishers
133 Chestnut Street
Amherst, MA 01002
USA

First Edition (Limited) 1998
ISBN 0-9641197-1-4

Clark, N. Laurie.
    It's Wesley!: the Adirondack guide / written and
illustrated by N. Laurie Clark. -- 1st ed. (limited)

    1. Praying mantis--Juvenile fiction. 2. Adirondack
Mountains (N.Y.)--Juvenile fiction. 3. Reincarnation--
Juvenile fiction. 4. Mountaineering guides (Persons)--
Juvenile fiction. I. Title.

PZ7.C54It 1998   813'.54[E]
                       QBI98-460

*Dedicated to Haley Elizabeth and
the future at Rugged Lake.*

"look at the strange fly on the window",
Larry pointed out as Mom and Lucy climbed
back into the car with their breakfast snack.

"Look at those huge claws, big eyes and wings. I'm going to squash him with my napkin!"

"No don't!", Mom yelled. "I think it's Wesley who's returned as a fly. He always said he'd come back to bother us. He's a good fly, a praying mantid - he catches and swallows bad bugs."

"What do you mean Mom? Tell us the story
about Wesley!", begged the kids.

.... "As a young man, Wesley was an Adirondack guide at Rugged Lake. Learned about the woods from his Grandpa, an Indian, so they say.

Fisherman and hunters from the big city paid money to stay at the Lodge. Wesley took care of all their needs and helped them with their 'catch'. They always went home with a deer or some trout.

Finally Rugged Lake became a Preserve, which meant Adirondack Guides could no longer be hired for hunting or fishing.

Wesley came to work for us at our camp that summer. He cut the wood for the stove, drove the truck to town for food supplies and rowed the boats across the lake. Wesley did a little bit of everything for us.

We were kids just like you then. Wesley even took us on canoe trips around Rugged Lake.

Wesley paddled us down to the Outlet where all the big rocks are. 'Boom, Pop'... up through the water came the otter, covered with lily pads. He'd stretch his head way up high to see who was coming. Otter was always on the lookout for beaver, his bitter enemy.

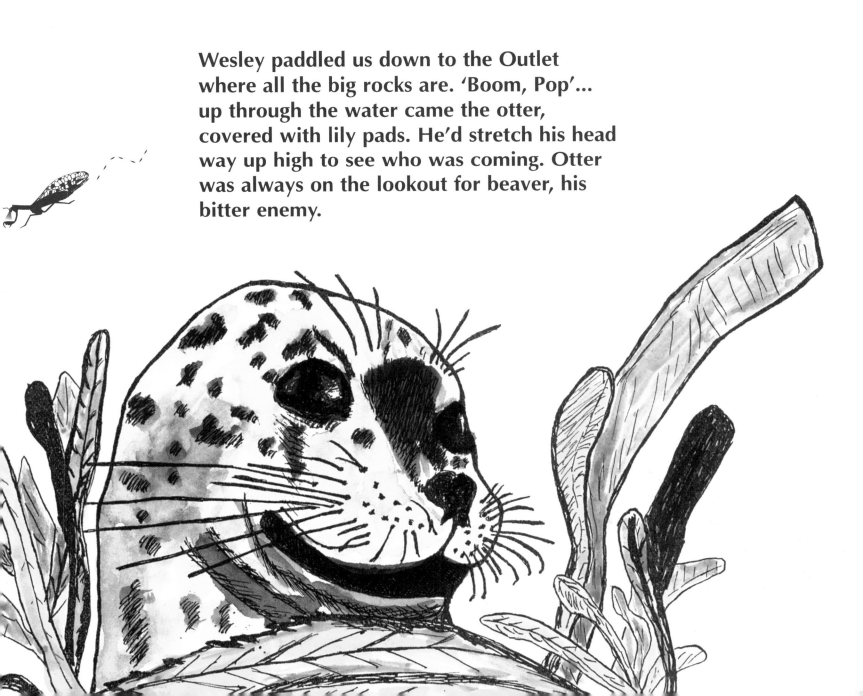

He'd show us the loon's nest down on Little Island. The loon chicks were learning how to dive for fish with Mama loon. Papa loon was always nearby trying to scare us away with his crazy yodel.

Wesley brought us home in time for a swim before dinner. We'd pass the Great Blue Heron, fishing along the shore. 'Plunk,' his head went under the water and up again with a fish in his beak which he'd swallow whole. His big wings flew him to the Upper Lake where he lived in a tall tree.

We even went out on the lake some nights.

The Great Grey Owl hooted his "hoo-hoo-whowho!" breaking the silence of the dark.

As the canoe moved under the shadow of Rugged Mounta Wesley directe his big lanter along the edge the shore. Suddenly we sa two deer, thei eyes reflecting t glow of the lig in their eyes. "Wow," we wh pered, just lou enough to scar the deer as the crashed off int the woods.

About the end of that summer, Wesley found the lost hikers on the back side of Mount Pinnacle. The couple had zig-zagged down off the trail by Lumber Camp Road at the upper end of the lake.

Wesley knew just where to find them. He rowed up the lake in his boat and found them asleep under a big tree. They were so happy to be rescued.

After that summer, Wesley went far away to work in the big city.

Wesley was gone a long, long time.

Finally, he came back to Rugged Lake as an old
man. Wesley did
all kinds of jobs around Camp for Grandy and Great Aunt Doris.
He cut wood for the stove, drove his truck to town for food supplies,
and rowed the boat across the lake.

Wesley did a little bit of everything
for us.

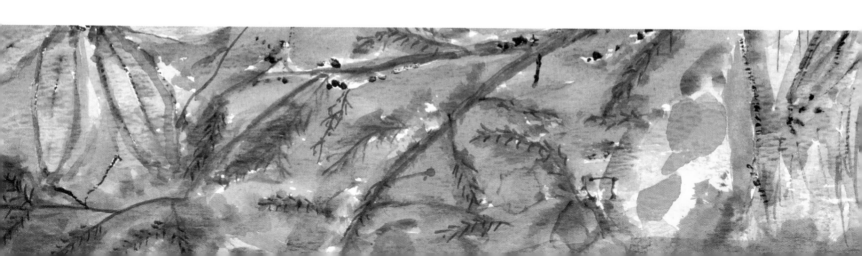

At night, we all sat around the big kitchen table and Wesley told us great stories of the 'old days.' We laughed at his hunting and fishing tales about deer, trout and the old folks with their Adirondack Guides.

We had such fun, except for the flies and bugs that were always biting and buzzing at us. 'Bang, swat, smash' would happen in the middle of Wesley's stories.

He didn't like these interruptions. He'd yell, "Leave those bugs alone! When I *come back* I'm going to be a fly to bother you and if I'm buzzing around your head, remember it's me - Wesley, your friend! I'll be there to help you..."

Mom never had time for more story-telling as we bounced down the rocky road to Rugged Lake.

"Oh, how beautiful," she exclaimed, "here's Camp in all its best Fall colors - bright red, yellow, gold and green!"

"We're here, we're here!" screamed Larry and Lucy as they looked across the lake in wonder. "We've *finally* arrived!".

Wesley, too, had turned into beautiful colors. He was *still* sitting on the window of the car as we pulled up to the boat house.

"There he goes," said Larry. "He's hungry - Look, he's flown off into the grass to catch some bugs."

"He's come back to Rugged Lake to be with us again!," replied Lucy with a smile.

Granny Lulu

Great Grandpa

Great Grandma

The author & artist

Mom

Larry & Lucy

Haley Elizabeth

For more information on other titles by N. Laurie Clark
or to order additional copies:

Write To:
Clark Publishers
133 Chestnut Street
Amherst, MA 01002
USA